בס"ד

The whole world is Hashem's, and all that is in it.

לה' הארץ ומלואה

RIYA

MY NAME

H. MANDEL

HACHAI PUBLISHING

RIVA

The Story of
DANNY
THREE TIMES

Written by **Leibel Estrin**

Illustrated by **Amir Zelcer**

Designed by **Ayala Stern**

Dedicated
to our dear children

David, Simcha & Daniel

from your parents
Roberta & Gabi Shabtai

Published by
HaChai Publishing

ISBN 0—922613—10—9 (Casebound Edition)
ISBN 0—922613—11—7 (Softcover Edition)

Distributed by:

HaChai Distributions
705 Foster Avenue
Brooklyn, New York 11230
(718) 692-3900

Typography by bp, Inc.
Printed in Hong Kong

This is the story of Danny Three Times.
DANNY: That's me!

He was called Danny Three Times
because his parents had to say everything
to him three times.

MOTHER: Danny, please come to dinner.

MOTHER: Danny, time for dinner.

(Mother to Danny . . . a little louder)
MOTHER: Danny!! Dinner!!!
DANNY: *(casually)* I'm coming, I'm coming.

Needless to say, the situation got so bad
that his parents were really upset.

BOTH PARENTS: We're really upset!

So they decided to take him to a child specialist.

FATHER: You're a child specialist?
DANNY: Of course!

FATHER: Our son never listens to us!

CHILD SPECIALIST: I see. *(Taking notes)*
MOTHER: So we have to say everything
   three times.

CHILD SPECIALIST: Go on. I'm listening.
FATHER: What do you suggest we do?
FATHER: I said, what do you think we
      should do?

FATHER: Excuse me! What do we do?!

CHILD SPECIALIST: Very simple! . . .
        Get used to it!
MOTHER & FATHER: Oh, no!

Next they asked his teacher.

TEACHER: Danny,
   be seated . . .
   that's strange.

Danny, please
be seated . . .
very strange.
I mean, that's
incredibly strange.

Danny, sit down!!!

They even tried a psychiatrist.

DOCTOR: I've checked him inside and out.
But I can't find anything wrong.
There's just one last possibility.

MOTHER: What's that?

DOCTOR: Do you give him fish to eat
        very often?
FATHER: Why? What does that have to do
        with anything?
DOCTOR: Well, maybe he is hard of *herring!*
        Hahahahaha!
FATHER: What?
DOCTOR: Sorry. That was just a little attempt
        at humor.
MOTHER: I would say a *very* little attempt
        at humor!

Finally they tried his rabbi.

RABBI: You know, the *mitzvah* of
honoring older people is very important.
And that's especially true of
honoring parents and teachers.
There must be a way to teach
that lesson to him. Hmm . . .
I think I know just how to do it!

The next day, Danny's parents put the rabbi's plan into action.

DANNY: Mom, may I please have peanut butter for lunch?

DANNY: Mom, may I please have peanut butter
for lunch?
MOTHER: *(Busy making something)*

DANNY: Mom, can I have peanut butter
      for lunch?
MOTHER: *(Still busy)*
DANNY: Mommie!!
      I want peanut butter, please!

MOTHER: I'm sorry, Danny,
      but I just made you a jelly sandwich.
      (Showing him the lunch she just made)

A few days later:

DANNY: Dad, I just blew up this beach ball.
Do you want to play catch?
FATHER: Sure, Danny. In a minute.

One minute soon passed. Then another.
And another.

DANNY: Dad, this ball has a leak in it! We have
to play before all the air goes out.
    (The ball starts to fizzle)
FATHER: O.K. I'll be right there.
DANNY: Dad! (Holding partly-inflated ball)
FATHER: I'm coming, I'm coming!

FATHER: Now, are you ready?
DANNY: Yea . . . I'm ready to do my homework.
    (Holding flat ball)

Later that evening:

DANNY: How come you never listen to me?

MOTHER: What?

FATHER: Say that again?

DANNY: See what I mean? You don't listen to me!

MOTHER: Sure we do. It's just that we don't think *you* listen to *us*!

DANNY: But I do hear you!
MOTHER: Then let's make a deal. We'll agree
to listen to you if you agree to listen to us!

FATHER: What do you think?
MOTHER: Do you agree?

    This time they didn't have to ask again.
Because Danny just smiled. And they knew.

MOTHER: Danny, dinner.
DANNY: I'm coming right now, Mom.